THIS CANDLEWICK BOOK BELONGS TO:

_____

_____

_____

To all the wonderful, mixed-up families
everywhere—the ones we're born into
and the ones we make along the way
A. K.

In memory of Philemon Sturges:
inspiration, mentor, and friend
B. K.

Text copyright © 2006 by Alethea Kontis
Illustrations copyright © 2006 by Bob Kolar

First paperback edition 2012

Library of Congress Cataloging-in-Publication
Data is available.

Library of Congress Catalog Card Number 2006042310

ISBN 978-0-7636-2728-7 (hardcover)
ISBN 978-0-7636-6084-0 (paperback)

18 19 20 21 22 APS 14 13 12 11 10

Printed in Humen, Dongguan, China

This book was typeset in Futura
and New Century Schoolbook.
The illustrations were created digitally.

Candlewick Press
99 Dover Street
Somerville, Massachusetts 02144

visit us at www.candlewick.com

Alpha Oops!

The Day Z Went First

Alethea Kontis   *illustrated by*

Bob Kolar

CANDLEWICK PRESS

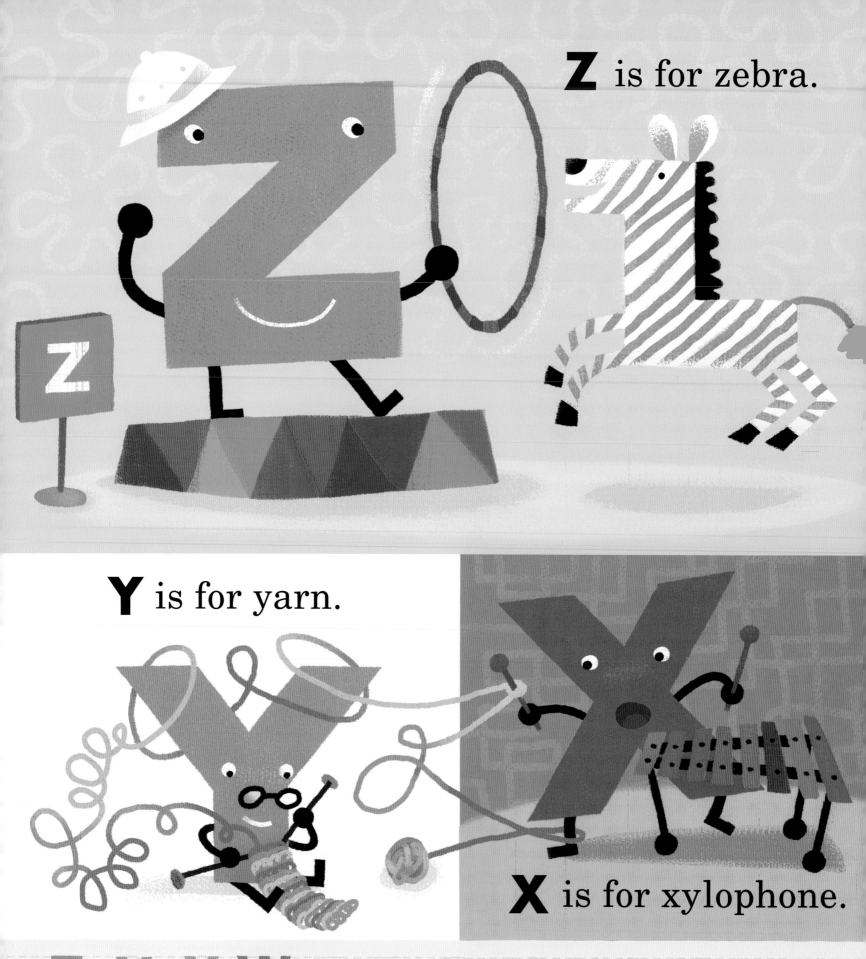

Z is for zebra.

Y is for yarn.

X is for xylophone.

W is for whale.

P is for penguins.

P! What do you think you're doing?

Oh, come on. Even if we go backwards, some of us are still stuck in the middle.

P is right.

Just because you all want to be different doesn't mean I do. I happen to like being right where I always am.

She's got a point.

S is for snake.

I is for insect.

V is for violin.

J is for jack-o'-lantern.

E is for Earth.

F is for flowers. And fairies.

Hey, I didn't get to pick two things.
I think I should get another turn.

I don't have much
to choose from.

No more turns!
You've had your turn.

Let someone else go.

Just move it along!

T is for taxi and train.

L is for lemons and lollipops.

K is for kangaroo and kites.

C is for cat and canary in cages.

Ooh, V is for violence.

R is for raindrops and rainbow.

D is for dragon and damsel in distress.

AZYXWPONHSIVJE

G is for green garden and great gorilla.

B is for big beautiful balloons blowing briskly in the breeze above a bevy of bright blue bouncing balls.

Oops.

B is also for broom.

M is for monster.

Q is for queen.

A Z Y X W P O N H S I V J E

Is that it? Am I last?

No, A's going to be last.

Is that everyone else, though?

I can't tell, now that we're all mixed up.

Has everyone had their turn?

F T L K C R D G B M X Y

Wait, Wait! U's been in the bathroom since
P took over. She missed the whole thing!

Do you still want me?

We're not complete without U!

Get up there, U!

U is for umbrella and unicorn.
And unique.

All right! That's everyone. We're ready for A.
A? Where are you?

I haven't seen her since H.

A is for apple, accident, accordion, acorn, acrobat, airplane, alligator, ambulance, anchor, angel, angle,

ant, Antarctica, archer, arrow, artichoke, artist, artwork, author, avenue, and ALPHABET.

F T L K C R D G B M Q U Z

Apology accepted.

F T L K C R D G B M Q U A

So we can all go back to normal now?

Yes. We should definitely go back to normal.

Z Y X W P O N H S I V J E

F T L K C R D G B M Q U A

Hey, Z? Next time just ask, okay?

Next time?

THE END

Alethea Kontis is the author of another book about the alphabet: *AlphaOops!: H Is for Halloween*. Of *AlphaOops!: The Day Z Went First*, she says, "I had a teacher tell me that when an author tries to come up with a character's name quickly, the brain starts with A, because that's the way we file things. My contrary brain said to itself, 'So, what if you filed things starting with Z? And hey, who asked the alphabet what order it wanted to be in, anyway?'"

Bob Kolar is the author-illustrator of *Do You Want to Play?*, *Racer Dogs*, and *Big Kicks* and the illustrator of *AlphaOops!: H Is for Halloween*, among other books. Of *AlphaOops!: The Day Z Went First*, he says, "I like having a K name, but I get tired of always being in the middle. I wish K was at the back with all the other cool letters: *A B C D E F G H I J L M N O P Q R S T U V W X Y Z K*—looks good to me." Bob Kolar lives in Kansas City, Missouri.